# GABRIELLE ROY

# THE TORTOISESHELL
## and the
# PEKINESE

**Illustrations by Jean-Yves Ahern**
**Translated by Patricia Claxton**

Copyright text © 1986 by Gabrielle Roy
Copyright illustration © 1986 by Jean-Yves Ahern
Copyright © 1989 translation by Patricia Claxton

All rights reserved

Typesetting: Southam Business Information
and Communications Group Inc.

*Canadian Cataloguing in Publication Data*

Roy, Gabrielle, 1909-1983
　[L'Espagnole et la Pékinoise.　English]
　The Tortoiseshell and the Pekinese

Translation of: L'Espagnole et la Pékinoise.
ISBN 0-385-25198-X

I. Ahern, Jean-Yves.　II. Title.　III. Title:
L'Espagnole et la Pékinoise.　English.

PS8535.O95E6813 1989　jC843'.54　C89-094064-9
PZ7.R68To 1989

Published by Doubleday Canada Limited
　　　　105 Bond Street
　　　　Toronto, Ontario
　　　　M5B 1Y3

Published in Québec by Les Éditions Du Boréal
　　　　5450, chemin de la Côte-des-Neiges
　　　　bureau 212
　　　　Montréal, Québec
　　　　H3T 1Y6

Printed and bound in the U.S.A.

# GABRIELLE ROY

# THE TORTOISESHELL
## and the
# PEKINESE

**Illustrations by Jean-Yves Ahern**
**Translated by Patricia Claxton**

Doubleday Canada Limited, Toronto

It happened without fail. Every time they met the insults would fly.

"*Phs-s-s-st!*" the cat would hiss. "I hate you, I hate you!"

"*Growr-r-r-r!*" the Pekinese would growl. "Ugly thing! Get out of my way. Go and lie down behind the stove."

"*You* go and lie down behind the stove. Ugly old thing yourself with your wrinkled-up face!"

Then Mei-Ling would give Lola a good clout with her paw. The cat would stagger from the blow.

"Do that once more and I'll scratch your eyes out," Lola would spit in Mei-Ling's face.

"Just you try and I'll choke you dead!"

Berthe would have to come and separate them.

"It's not nice, not nice at all! Two animals living in the same house and they can't get along for one minute!"

Once, at Christmas, she had tried to get them to shake paws and be friends. Never had they scratched at one another and bitten each others' ears more savagely.

Eventually, in order to have some peace and quiet, Berthe would send each of them to a different part of the house.

"Mei-Ling, get behind the stove! Go along now!"

The cat would taunt in the same tone of voice, "Mei-Ling, get behind the stove! Go along now!"

And to rub it in she would add, "I told you to get behind the stove, so there!"

But then it would be her own turn for punishment.

"Lola, up to the attic, and I don't want to hear another sound from you."

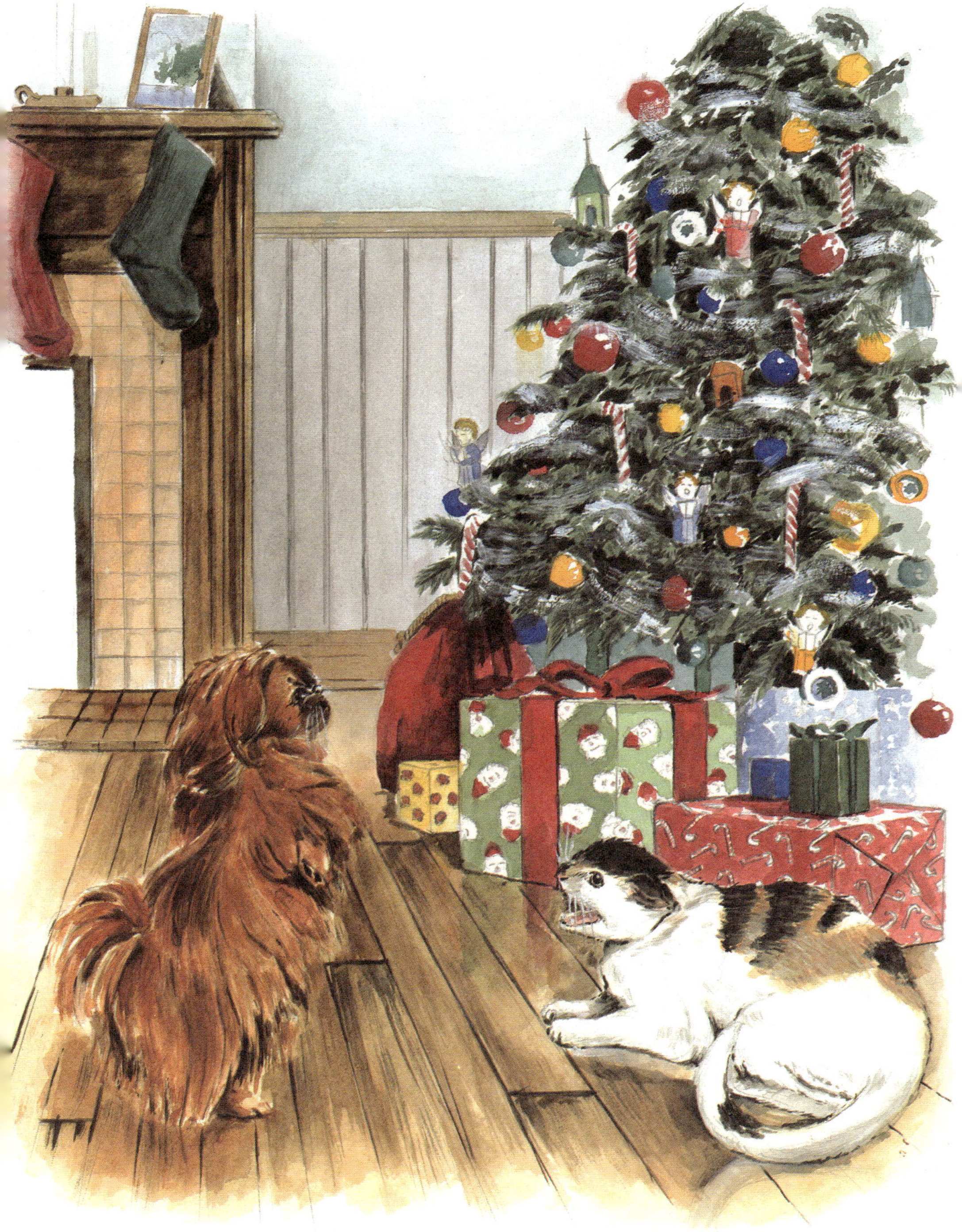

With her head down, Mei-Ling would slink into the narrow space behind the stove, muttering her own taunt:

"Lola, up to the attic! You asked for it."

The stairs were short and steep, leading from the small summer kitchen, which was called the "old house", up to the tiny attic above through a trap door which was never closed.

Lola went to the attic without being told twice. She rather liked being there in fact. The heat from the stove pipe passing through made it cosy and warm. There was even a small bed for resting on in the daytime.

But to show her independence, she stopped briefly on the second to last step. Here she was close enough for a quick retreat to territory that was forbidden to Mei-Ling, in case the dog took it into her head to give chase. Besides, up here she had a good view of Mei-Ling doing penance behind the stove. From this vantage point, paws tucked underneath her and head resting on the edge of the step, she could jeer in safety.

"You're gross! Greedy, rude, revolting, just like all dogs! Stop-and-sniff-at-every-tree. Leave-your-mess-where-all-can-see!"

Tired to death of hearing the same things day after day, Mei-Ling would stop answering and turn to lie on her other side, her back to Lola. Trying to cover her ears with her paws, she would mutter:

"That's enough, let me sleep now. Two-faced cat!"

At mealtimes it was even worse. Berthe had to serve their food in their own separate dishes, and what is more, put them down in opposite corners of the kitchen.

Even so, Lola hardly ever had time to finish what she had in her own dish. She would eat delicately, carefully choosing what she liked best from the mixture of odds and ends and leaving the least appetizing until last. Mei-Ling, meanwhile, would gobble whatever was closest to her mouth and all together, sweet and salty, pickles and milk. She almost always finished long before Lola. Then she would come and take whatever the cat still had left in her dish.

"Move over and get lost," she would growl softly so Berthe wouldn't overhear.

Though she might still be pretty hungry, the cat would give up her place at the dish. She couldn't fight to keep her food and eat at the same time.

Sometimes, as she watched from a distance, tears would come to her eyes to see the remains of her meal being bolted by the dog. Specially when the remains happened to be fish. Sometimes, quietly, she would creep close. Then she would dart out a paw, trying to take back at least one piece of the stolen food. With her mouth full, Mei-Ling would growl, "Don't you dare, or you'll see what a thrashing you'll get."

As time went on, however, the war between the two seemed to grow less intense. The cat was gaining weight. Her stomach swelled. She would still mutter insults at Mei-Ling when their paths crossed, but really nothing much. It seemed that her mind was occupied with something other than quarreling. She would often go to the attic of her own accord and rest for hours on end. Though she wouldn't have admitted this, Mei-Ling was rather lonesome. She was almost happy to see that stuck-up cat come downstairs once in a while. Berthe would now go to the refrigerator just for Lola. She would

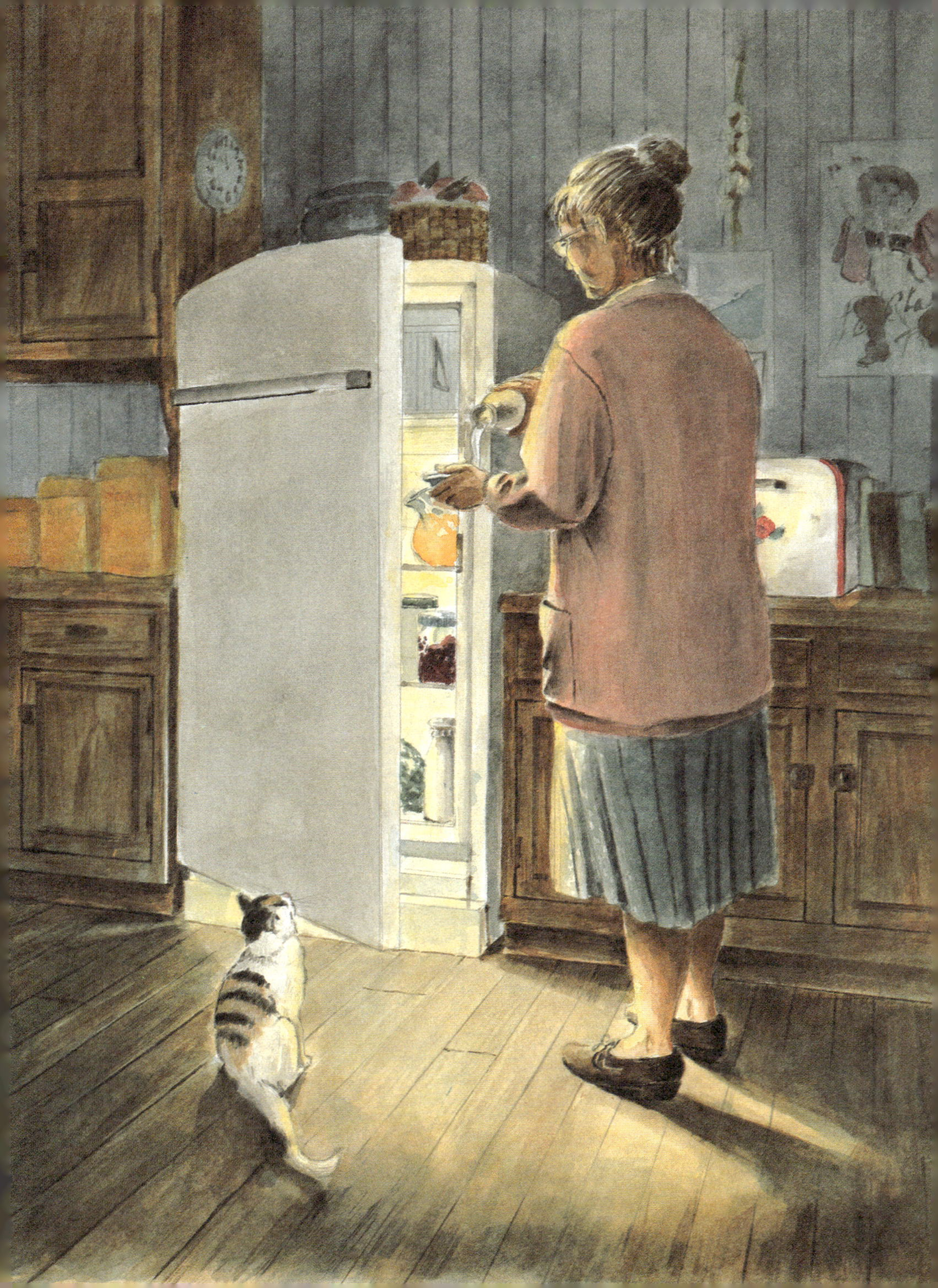

pour her a saucer of milk and not allow Mei-Ling a single drop.

Then one night there was a commotion. Lola came downstairs awkwardly, not in leaps barely touching the steps as she usually did. She came and spoke quietly to Berthe who stroked her head and carried her back upstairs. Mei-Ling heard a lot of walking around and things being moved up there. Berthe came downstairs and went right back up with a big saucer of milk. Room service in the attic now, if you please! Mei-Ling retreated behind the stove to sulk, thinking there was no mistake who was the favourite any more.

She couldn't sleep. Jealousy was not the only thing gnawing at her. Curiosity was consuming her too. To begin with, why had Lola got so fat? Why was her personality so different? And what could she have been doing up in the attic all this time?

Mei-Ling went to the bottom of the stairs and listened. She heard nothing. She began to climb the stairs in her clumsy way. They were

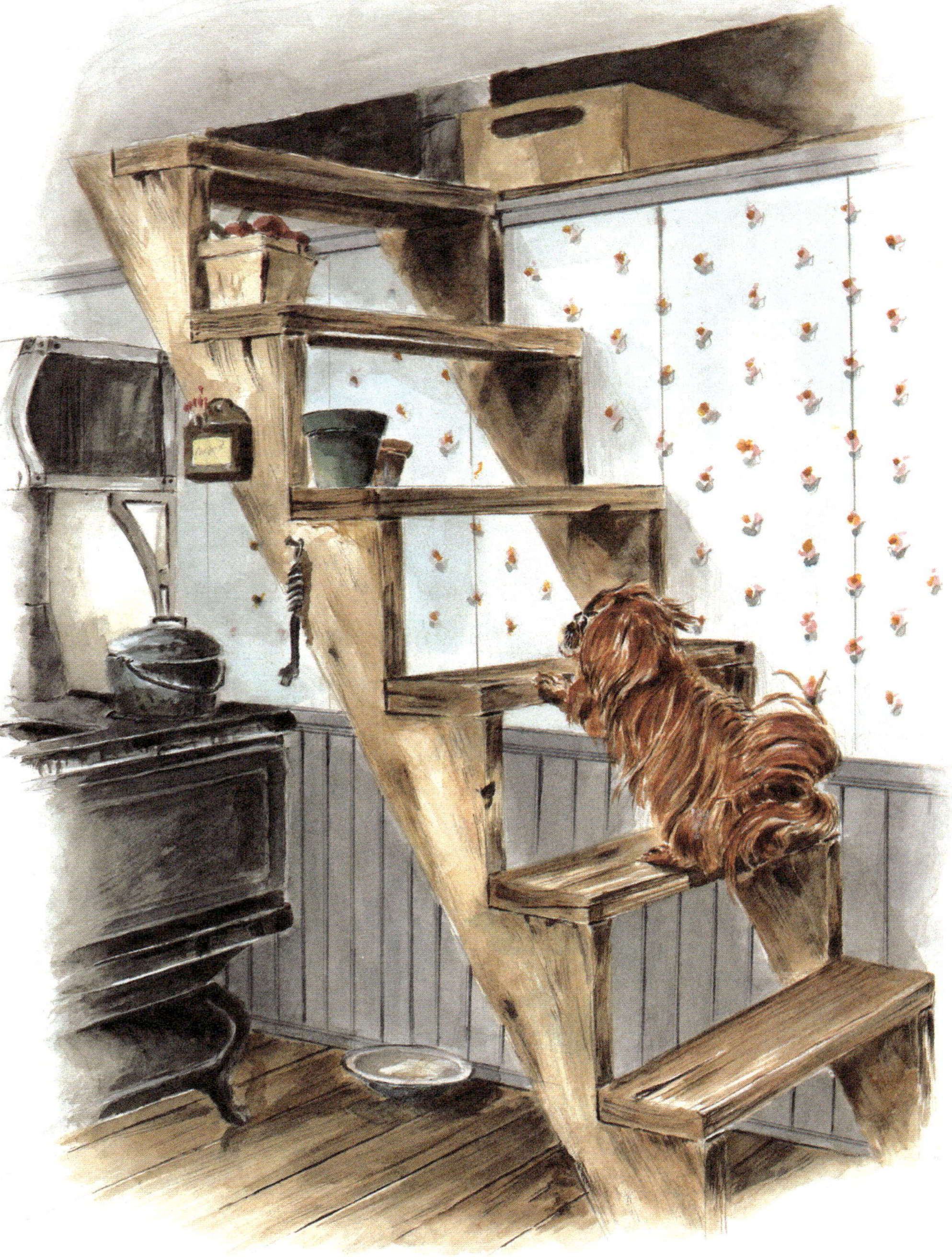

very steep for her short legs. She stopped on the second to last step. She had rarely disobeyed the rule about staying out of the attic when Lola was there. Each had her special place. Mei-Ling's was the narrow space behind the stove, usually a good place in winter, though not so good when Berthe made the fire in the stove too hot. That stupid cat had the best of it of course, a whole comfortable attic to herself.

There on the second to last step, Mei-Ling listened very, very carefully. She thought she heard the strange sound the cat would make when her mistress stroked her, for example. Why would she be making that noise now, all alone in the dark?

Mei-Ling couldn't resist any longer. She climbed to the last step. A moonbeam shining through the window was giving some light to the attic. There was a big cardboard box in the middle of the room. Lola's face was visible over its edge. It wasn't her usual, hateful face. It made one think she was trying to be friendly, or perhaps even that she was afraid. Sitting half crouched she asked:

"You haven't come here to make trouble, have you?"

Her manner had changed so much that Mei-Ling, astonished, changed her own manner almost against her will. Could this be how gentleness sometimes wins on Earth?

Mei-Ling gave a little growl anyway, but just pretend, not really an angry growl. She came closer, rose on her back feet and put her front paws on the edge of the box. What she saw inside was such a surprise she gave a sound like "oooh!" She couldn't say another word, or move a hair, all because of the sight before her eyes.

Now Berthe appeared from the other part of the house, through the passage leading from her bedroom to the little attic. She had thought she heard Mei-Ling's claws on the wooden stairs and had hurried in, worried for Lola's safety.

Seeing Mei-Ling's head inside the box,

she was about to cry out, "Take care not to hurt the kittens!", but stopped herself just in time.

She stopped because the little dog looked up. Berthe could see Mei-Ling's eyes in the light of the moon shining through the window. They were filled with a kind of love she had never seen there before. Until now she had seen Mei-Ling's love for her, and occasionally for other humans. What she was seeing now was different: love of one animal for other animals. A love that was almost as radiant as the moonlight pouring into the attic.

Mei-Ling, her head once again inside the box, seemed unable to recover from her surprise. Besides, when the three kittens were so much like their mother — whom Mei-Ling had always thought as ugly as sin — why did she find them so beautiful?

Then, a quiet, warm, friendly conversation full of goodwill began between the two

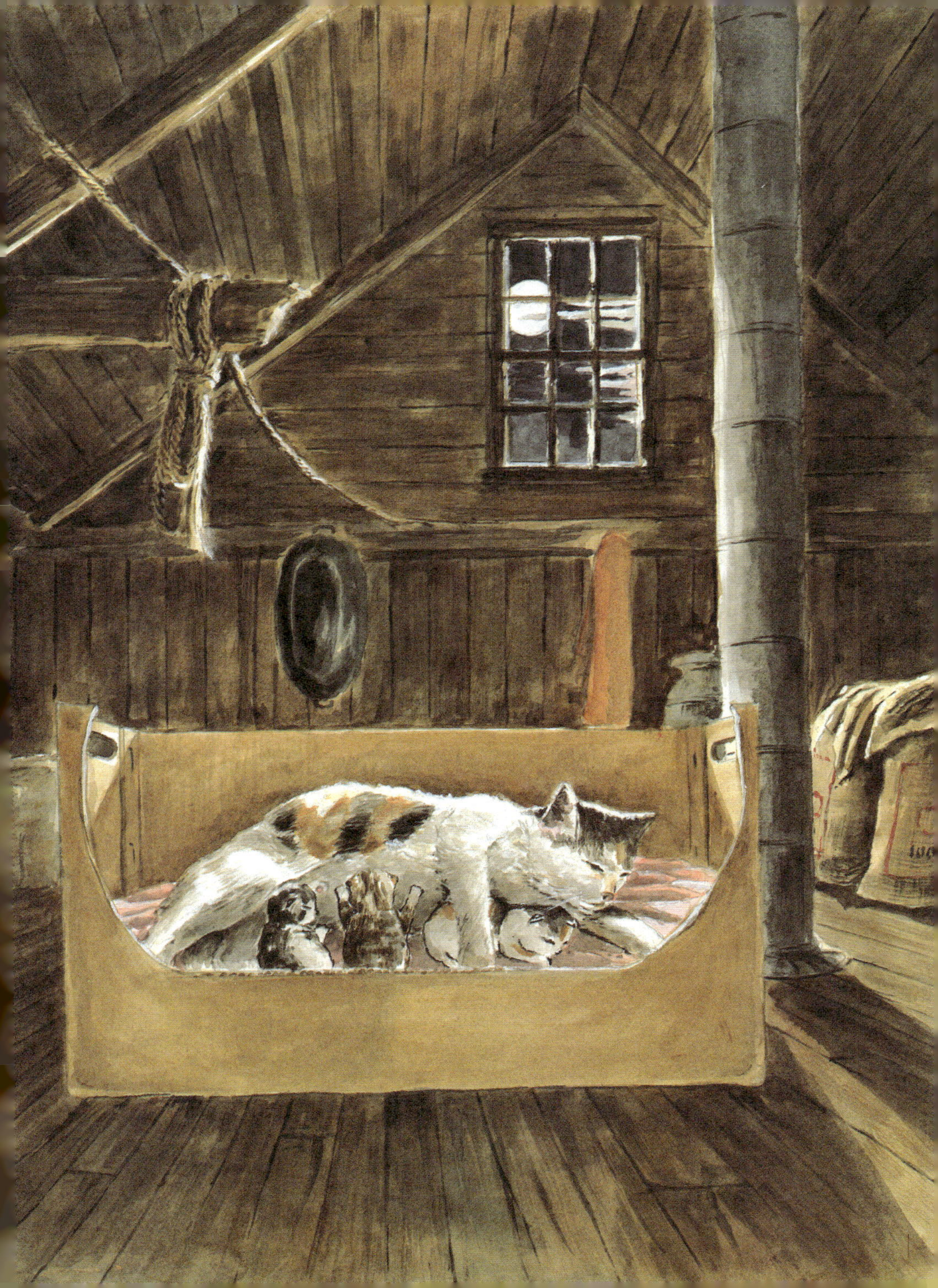

animals who yesterday had been unable to abide each other.

Mei-Ling seemed to be asking questions.

"Are they yours?"

"Of course."

"You made them yourself?"

"Who else do you suppose made them?" retorted the cat, though without a hint of the scorn she had always shown before. "Of course I did. They're my children."

A little later she asked, "Haven't you ever had children of your own?"

A shadow crossed Mei-Ling's wrinkled face. She searched inside her head. To tell the truth she didn't really know what she was searching for.

"I guess I've not," she replied at last. "If I'd had any I'd remember. You wouldn't forget children if you'd had them."

"I should hope not!" said Lola.

As if she were a queen, there with her children around her in the old cardboard box made to hold lard, she continued:

"How come you never had any puppies?"

Mei-Ling's eyes wandered rather wistfully. She couldn't have known that she had been operated on to prevent her from having children and so had not had any and never would. This was to protect her from the advances of big, rough male dogs. It was also meant to keep peace on the farm, for when the male dogs came courting from miles around there would surely have been fights to decide which one of them would have her as his bride.

Mei-Ling's eyes were round and moist as she thought and thought, not finding the reason why such happiness had escaped her. At last she said humbly:

"You have three. Wouldn't you lend me one?"

"Are you crazy?" exclaimed Lola. "If you ask such a thing you certainly can't have had any children yourself."

"It would just be for an hour or two," Mei-Ling pleaded. "I'd bring it back."

Lola softened.

"No, I don't lend my children. I'll let you come and look at them sometimes, though. But be careful you don't hurt them with your big clumsy paws."

"I'll be very careful," promised Mei-Ling.

Then she heaved a sigh.

"Well, good night now," she said,

". . . since you don't want me to help you." And she went down the stairs and to bed all alone behind the stove.

Berthe tiptoed away. Lola purred her children to sleep. And Mei-Ling had a beautiful dream. She dreamed she was in a big cardboard lard box with eight puppies all like her, brown faces and the rest covered with long rust-coloured fur. And they were all cuddled up to her the way Lola's children were with their mother.

Although Mei-Ling longed to be visiting in the attic at all hours of the day, most often she hung back when the cat was there. But the minute Lola left to go hunting or to do her business, Mei-Ling would scamper up the stairs. Not as Lola would, with her paws barely touching the steps as she went, but pretty fast for a little dog with slippery claws.

She would jump into the lard box, half squashing the kittens with her weight, and try to behave like the cat. She would curl her paw around the kittens as she had seen Lola do. She would wag her tail. She would lick the kittens' faces and ears. But the kittens would try to nurse and find no milk, just fur on her stomach. They would be angry. Then she would try to calm them with what she thought was purring. The best she could do was a *rowrr-rowrr-rowrr* that frightened the children. Yet they became used to this peculiar mother who appeared out of the blue the minute their own had left. They were soon playing happily, tugging at the hair on her ears, pulling her eyebrows and nipping at her lips.

   Blissfully, she let it all happen. Lying on her back with her paws in the air, filling the box herself almost completely, she would give her *rowrr-rowrr-rowrr* to amuse the little ones, who would be climbing about on her head since there was no other room in the box.

   One day Lola appeared unexpectedly to find them all frolicking this way together. She nearly lost her temper, but Mei-Ling looked so comical upside down she decided to laugh instead.

Whenever visitors came, Berthe liked to show off the kittens. She would go to the attic and bring down the cats' house. Lola would come down beside her, grumbling:

"I don't like my children being dragged around. I don't like them being shown to strangers."

But Berthe would take the three kittens out of their house. She would put them on the floor to see them trying to walk. They would totter about on their tiny limbs. Their back legs would collapse under them, they would get up and then fall over again. Lola would show that she was anxious. She kept making strange, throaty sounds which must have been warnings of a kind.

"Don't go too far. Whatever you do, don't go under the big cupboard with short legs or we'll never be able to get you out."

But that is exactly where they did go.

"I told you so, I told you so," their mother would wail.

The time has come for me to explain that this cat called Lola, such a very Spanish name, was no more Spanish than you or I. No more than Mei-Ling, the Pekinese, was Chinese. Lola was a tortoiseshell cat, which doesn't mean she wore a tortoiseshell either, or was even related to a tortoise. She simply had black, white and yellow fur in a tortoiseshell pattern. This is rather rare, which is why these cats are prized. It happened that one of the kittens was a tortoiseshell, the image of his mother. He was the kitten everyone wanted.

"I'll take him," said a cousin of Berthe's.

"No," said Berthe, "I'm keeping that one. Choose another."

"Please let me have it," begged the

cousin. "I'll keep one of my Persian kittens for you in exchange."

This bargaining was the last straw for Lola. She tried to bring her children back to their house, but they had wandered off to the far corners of the kitchen. She had more than her paws full rounding them up. While she held one, the other two would escape again. Then Mei-Ling came to help. She stood

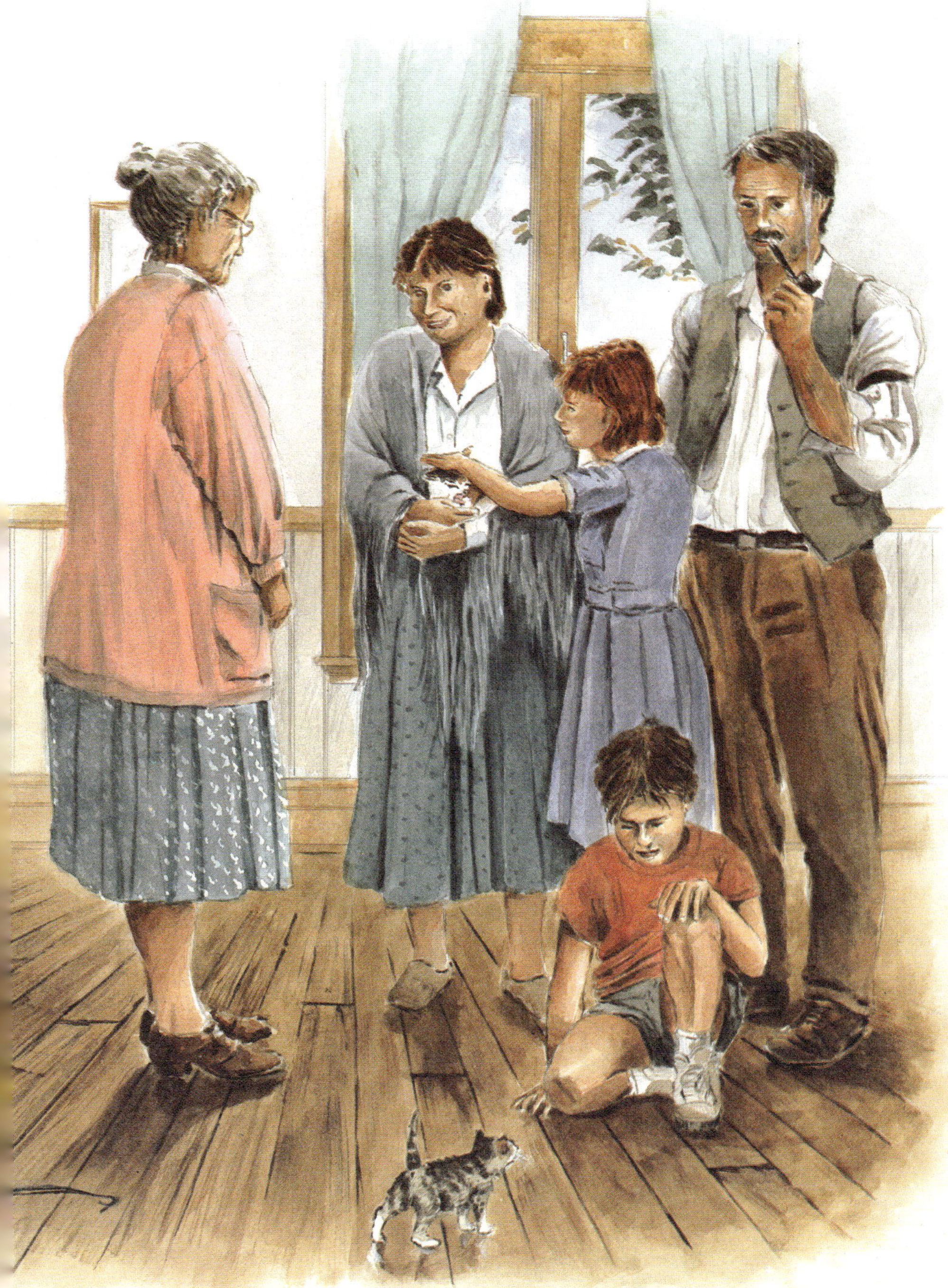

blocking the kittens' way, which gave Lola a chance to catch them. Between the two, they succeeded in bringing all of them back to the box. Lola jumped inside and Mei-Ling lifted the kittens in one by one. She had learned from Lola how to hold them without closing her teeth too tight.

Thanks to the dog, Lola was finally safe at home with all her children. Gracious for the first time in her life, she nodded her head like a grand Spanish lady and said very distinctly:

"Thank you. You're very kind."

"Don't mention it," replied Mei-Ling, just as politely.

Not long after this, Berthe carried the box back up to the attic, accompanied by Lola and Mei-Ling.

In the attic together, the two mothers came to the conclusion that they must do everything possible to save the family. Danger had been too close for comfort. Lola was still trembling.

"It always starts this way," Lola confided to the Pekinese. "They steal one of my kittens when I'm not looking. 'She won't notice,' they say. They think I can't count. Then a few days later they take another."

"We won't let them," said the Pekinese.

She went to the edge of the trap door to stand guard, teeth bared.

"If they come they'll have to deal with me!"

"Even the two of us together can't stop them from taking our children," said Lola. "There's only one thing to do. We must leave."

In the end they decided to make their move that very night. All the people in the house were gathered in front of the television watching a man on the moon. There wouldn't be another opportunity like this for a long time. It was rare for the coast to be so clear.

Lola began by lifting Black-and-White out of the box.

Mei-Ling came and took him from her by the scruff of his neck.

"Where are we going?" she asked out of the corner of her mouth.

"At the edge of the porch there's a hole that leads under the floor of the old house. There's room at the middle for all five of us to live in."

"Will I get through the hole?" asked Mei-Ling anxiously.

"If you pull in your stomach a bit, yes, I think so. I'll show you how to stretch out and make yourself thin."

Working together, they had soon brought the three children downstairs. In the next room the family was still glued to the television set. "Did you see?" exclaimed a voice. "Man has really set foot on the moon! It's just

unbelievable what we're seeing in our day."
The whole house could have been moved complete with the people in it before any of them would have noticed.

Mei-Ling knew how to open the screen door. She held it open while Lola went back and forth, taking out one kitten after the other and putting it on the porch.

In less than half an hour they were comfortably settled in a kind of cave dug in the earth. There was some daylight coming through holes made by fieldmice. Mei-Ling had had some difficulty squeezing through the main entrance, but she had managed, and all she had left behind were a few hairs.

Soon they heard footsteps overhead. The man was going to stay on the moon for the night and the family were coming back to the kitchen to talk some more about what they had seen.

Berthe had no doubt been to the attic and discovered that the animals had fled.

Listening through the floor, Lola and Mei-Ling knew very well that the conversation was about them.

"They might have gone into the woods, the way Cliptail did years ago," said Berthe's brother, Aimé.

"Oh no! Lola wouldn't be up to that."

"Still," said Berthe, who was beginning to see the light, "you'd be surprised what she can do. Specially if she has help."

The cat and the dog looked at each other. They wanted so much to laugh, their faces were all creased.

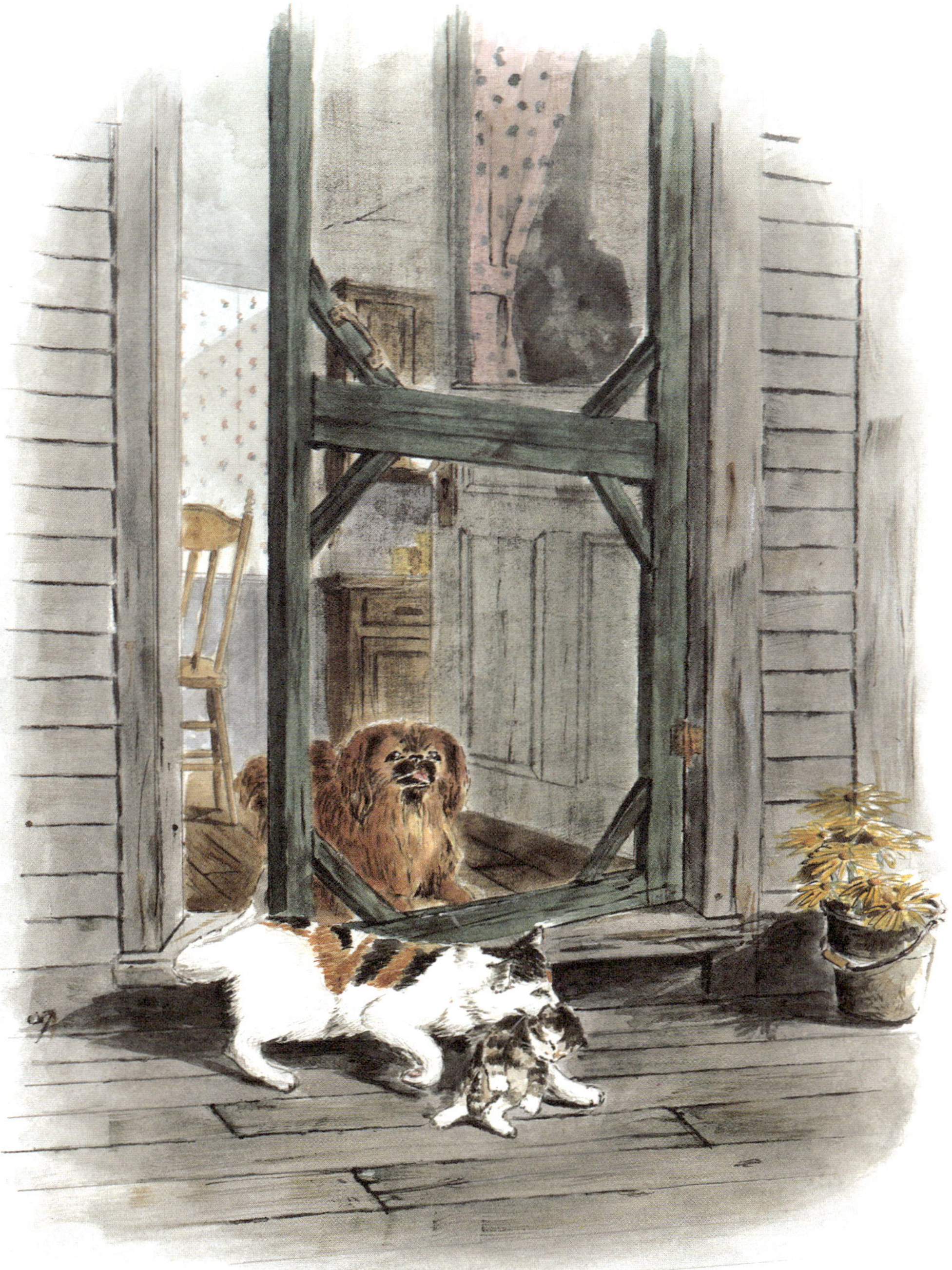

The kittens grew fast. Before long they found their way out from under the house. Because they had been raised there and liked it, they didn't dream of running away. They stayed on or near the porch to play. It was midsummer. They spent whole days making up new games. Sometimes with their cat mother, sometimes with their dog mother. For them, there was no difference between the two. Except that one gave milk and the other gave boundless love. For games, they even almost preferred the little dog. She would roll on her back with her feet in the air, jump up again and yap in their faces in friendly excitement, or, taking care not to bite them, let them climb almost whole into her mouth. It was comical.

There were lovely summer evenings which everybody spent outdoors. The people would sit in their rocking chairs on the porch. They would breathe the scent of the tall stalks in the garden. Lola and Mei-Ling would sometimes get tired and come to sit nearby on the porch steps, talking together of this and that. They would watch their children continue to frisk and play. The kittens would leap in the air with all four feet off the ground, bounding sideways several times in succession. Or they'd pounce on each other, one trying to roll the other over on the ground.

The people on the porch watched the games with as much interest as the kittens' mothers.

By agreement, Lola and Mei-Ling would return to the fray all of a sudden. They had invented a game rather like baseball. Mei-Ling would take her place near the edge of the small vegetable garden and Lola would go to the other side of the yard near a rock. They would stand facing each other and then, at a signal given by one of them, everyone would run around in a circle. Clockwise first, then in the opposite direction. The aim was apparently to be the first to arrive at a place left unoccupied.

In the end, none of it looked like any game anyone knew. The cat chased the dog.

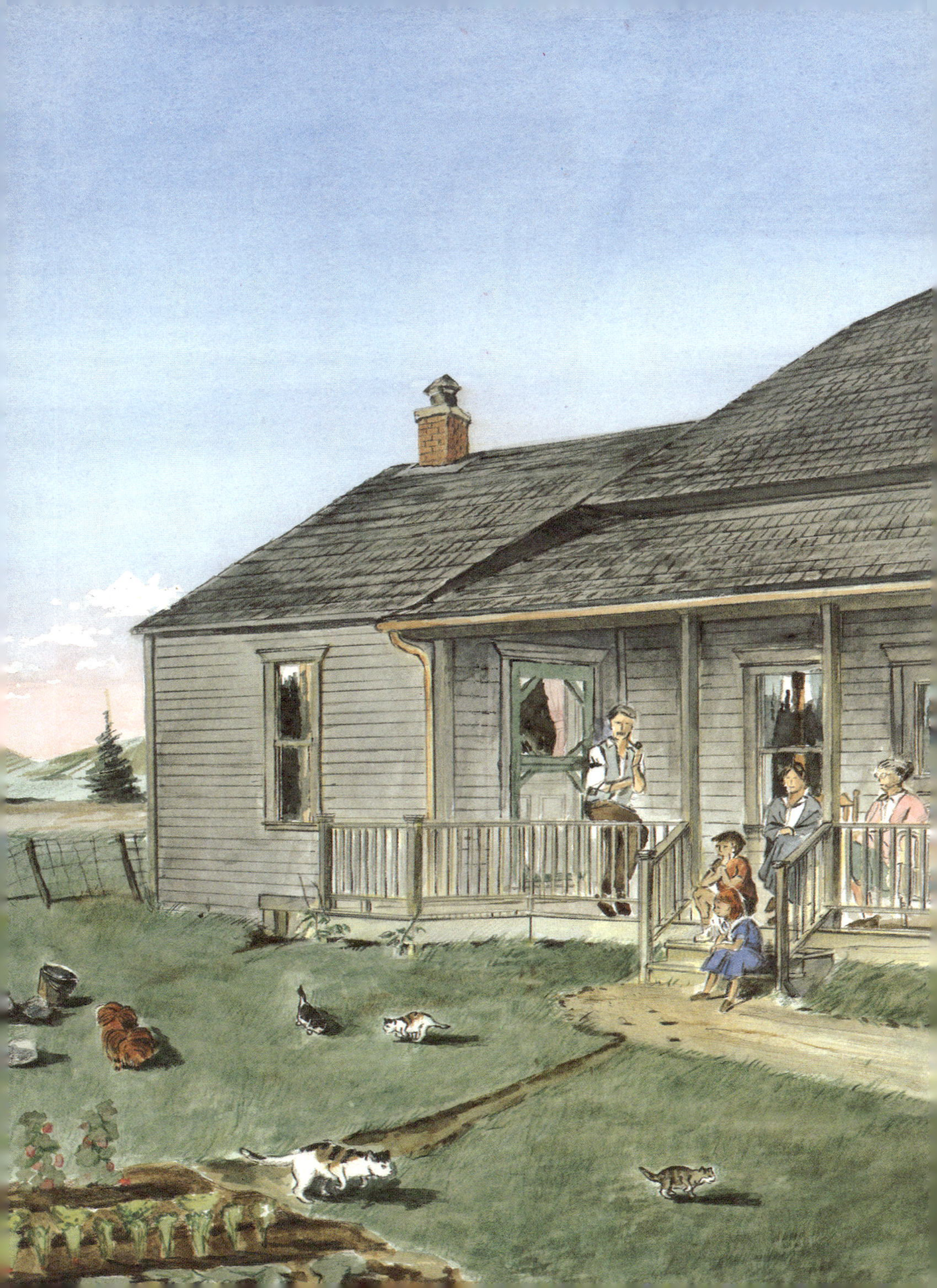

The dog, tail between her legs, pretended to be frightened. The little ones attacked the grownups. The grownups ran as if the devil were on their tails.

So it would go until they were all worn out and collapsed in a heap together, asleep with their paws intertwined.

Berthe, rocking on the porch, said one day:

"They're children who have made peace. Perhaps one day all children on Earth will join hands. Then there will be no more fighting, ever again."

# GABRIELLE ROY
## 1909-1983

Gabrielle Roy was born in Saint-Boniface, Manitoba on March 22, 1909. She was a schoolteacher for ten years, an experience which later inspired some of her best writing. Immediately prior to the Second World War she spent two years in Europe, after which she settled in Montreal where, as a freelance journalist, she published her early stories and articles. Her first novel, *Bonheur d'occasion*, won wide acclaim in France, where it won the prestigious Prix Femina, as well as in the United States and Canada, and has been translated into 14 languages. Its English translation, *The Tin Flute*, was chosen as a Book of the Month by the Literary Guild of America. She wrote her second novel, *La Petite Poule d'Eau* (*Where Nests the Water Hen*), during an extended stay in France with her husband, Dr. Marcel Carbotte. It was published in 1950, and thereafter the author lived in relative seclusion in Quebec City and at her summer cottage at Petite-Rivière-Saint-François, writing novels, articles, short stories, children's books and finally an autobiography, *La détresse et l'enchantement* (Enchantment and Sorrow), which was published posthumously. All have been hailed as highly personal and sensitive works offering a deeply compassionate vision of life, and marked by yearning for universal understanding. Gabrielle Roy received many honours in Canada and abroad for her writing. She died on July 13, 1983.

*The Tortoiseshell and the Pekinese*, entitled *L'Espagnole et la Pékinoise* in French, was originally written in the early 1970s and was revised and made ready for publication by the author some years later. It was found among her papers after her death and appeared for the first time in 1986 in French.

# THE WORKS OF GABRIELLE ROY

*Bonheur d'occasion* (*The Tin Flute*, trans. Hannah Josephson; retrans. Alan Brown), novel.
*La Petite Poule d'Eau* (*Where Nests the Water Hen*, trans. Harry Binsse), novel.
*Alexandre Chenevert* (*The Cashier*, trans. Harry Binsse), novel.
*Rue Deschambault* (*Street of Riches*, trans. Harry Binsse), novel.
*La Montagne secrète* (*The Hidden Mountain*, trans. Harry Binsse), novel.
*La Route d'Altamont* (*The Road Past Altamont*, trans. Joyce Marshall), novel.
*La Rivière sans repos* (*Windflower*, trans. Joyce Marshall), novel.
*Cet été qui chantait* (*Enchanted Summer*, trans. Joyce Marshall), short stories.
*Un jardin au bout du monde* (*Garden in the Wind*, trans. Alan Brown), short stories.
*Ma Vache Bossie* (*My Cow Bossie*, trans. Alan Brown), children's story.
*Ces enfants de ma vie* (*Children of My Heart*, trans. Alan Brown), novel.
*Fragiles lumières de la Terre* (*The Fragile Lights of Earth*, trans. Alan Brown), essays.
*Courte-Queue* (*Cliptail*, trans. Alan Brown), children's story.
*De quoi t'ennuies-tu, Evelyne? suivi de Ely! Ely! Ely!* (English translation pending), short stories.
*L'Espagnole et la Pékinoise* (*The Tortoiseshell and the Pekinese*, trans. Patricia Claxton), children's story.
*La détresse et l'enchantement,* (*Enchantment and Sorrow*, trans. Patricia Claxton), autobiography.
*Ma chère petite soeur: lettres à Bernadette* (English translation pending), letters.

# JEAN-YVES AHERN

Jean-Yves Ahern is a graduate of the National Theatre School (Set Design, 1982). He gained experience through a number of theatre productions as a technician, and shortly began designing sets at the Café-théâtre de l'Avant-scène and the Salle Calixa-Lavallée in Montreal. He participated in the production of the films *Hold-up* and *Night Magic* as illustrator and conceptionist. His work has also included architectural drawing and interior design. Jean-Yves Ahern's last illustrations for children appeared in *La Bicyclette volée*, published by Editions etudes vivantes.